EMBRACING (

SHINE

By

ALISSA FRANCA

Dedication

I dedicate this book to my parents Nada and Frank, who believed in me every step of the way.

Acknowledgement

Thank you to my wonderful team at The Global Publishers for your guidance and support during this journey.

To my loved ones, thank you for pushing me to believe in myself. Your love and support are what inspired me to finally complete and publish this story after all of these years.

Table of Contents

CHAPTER ONE

ETHAN

I could hear his voice. Coming closer. Coming to me.

Hide, I thought.

But where?

I was cornered. Nowhere to go. Nowhere to run. Nowhere to hide.

A deep laugh echoed around me, snapping me out of my thoughts.

He found me.

I closed my eyes.

"Yo! Stutter Boy," he called out.

Go away. Please.

"Why are your eyes closed, Stutter Boy? Are you going to cry, Stutter Boy? You know we might not hurt you so bad if you start crying." It was another voice.

"Maybe he's already crying," he snickered.

Please, I thought desperately. Leave me alone.

When I opened my eyes, I saw him and his two burly friends flanked on either side of him. I knew them from school. All three of them were stocky giants with arms the size of cannonballs and eyes that contained fire.

His dark, steady eyes pierced through my brain. He was the tallest of them all, wide-shouldered and muscular, a menacing grin plastered upon his face.

They stalked towards me, and I quickly backed up until I felt the cold, stone wall against my back.

"I saw your mom at the bar, Stutter Boy," he said.

"She's hot." It was one of his friends, the shortest one with a tattoo of a snarling pit bull on his forearm, who was talking.

"I didn't know she was a dancer; how many guys does she get with a night? Five? Ten?" he asked.

He waited for my response, arms crossed, sly grin, knowing I would snap.

And I did.

"My-y m-mom i-ss not-t a-a danc-cer" I struggled to say, "Sh-he is-s a-a bar-tt-end-er."

They all laughed, and for a split second I imagined them as the three hyenas in the Lion King, all equally ugly and stupid but sickeningly evil and scary.

He grinned at me, "I know she's a bar-tt-end-eerr." The other two laughed at his impersonation of me. I just stood there waiting for him to beat me up already. "But she must do other things for tips," he paused to snicker. "If you know what I mean."

I could feel the heat rising to my face as it consumed my entire body. My vision turned red. I clenched my hand into a fist but kept it at my side.

He winked, "Alright, Stutter Boy. It's beating time."

What did I do to deserve this?

Had I done something wrong?

I tried to think of the answer as a fist slammed into my chest.

I tried to protect my face with my hand when I felt one of them grab onto my jacket as he slammed my body into the ground. My vision started to blur; everything started spinning. Liquid smacked my face—spit. I didn't have time to wipe it off. He pinned me down and sat on my chest. My lungs burned.

"Stop fighting." He ordered between gritted teeth.

I continued to shove him off of me. I watched as he lifted his clenched fist, and he punched me. Hard. Again, and again, and again. Pain jolted through my body, making my bones quiver. I felt something gooey run out of my nose, blood.

"S-S-Stop." I gasped just as a foot connected against my back.

Someone snickered, and a hand covered my mouth.

"SHUT UP!" he ordered.

I did. I had no choice. They were too strong. I was too weak. "I will not cry," I told myself. I will not scream, I told myself. "I will not talk," I told myself.

And I didn't.

"See ya at school, Stutter Boy!" one of them shouted. I felt the person that was sitting on me stand up; my lungs gasped for air. I let out loud, vicious coughs. The sound of heavy footsteps and laughter echoed down the alleyway until I could only hear my own ragged breathing. Slowly, I attempted to raise my head off the ground, but my neck buckled, and it hit the pavement. Defeated, I closed my eyes and began to cry.

****

When I got home the streetlights were shining, cutting through the dark sky. My mom was still at work; her shift usually ended at around three in the morning. I was used to being home by myself at night. My house was on the corner of the long, narrow street, next to the gas station and the forest where the druggies go to have fun. It was old, the roof was starting to fall apart, and the windows were cracked. But it was something to live in. It was a tiny bungalow, with only one floor, one bedroom, a rundown kitchen, one bathroom, and a small living area where our couch was placed. My mom and I alternate every night between the room and the couch. That night was my turn in the room.

I made my way into the bedroom and stared at myself in the mirror; layers of dust covered the glass, but it was clear enough to use. My mom and I try our best to keep the place clean, but it gets hard with her work schedule and my homework. As I couldn't help but wince at how dishevelled I looked. My eyes gazed at the reflection in the mirror. My dark hair was a tangled mess, and my upper lip was oozing with hot blood; the bruise covering my left eye was a mixture of blue and black. I looked like I just stepped out of an action movie, like the hero who would look badass and dangerous. Which was the opposite of how I felt. I wanted to vomit. I wanted to cry. And most of all, I just wanted to sleep. Tears streamed down my cheeks; I didn't stop them. I let myself cry. A teardrop touched my lip, and I tasted the salt as it burned my cut.

As I watched myself cry, the home phone rang. I slowly limped over and answered it.

"H-hello?" I tried my best to control my voice.

"Hi honey." It was my mom; I recognized her voice, high-pitched like a young girl's. "How was school today?" The sound of drunk laughter and clanging glasses vibrated through the phone.

I winced. "I-I-t," I paused to give myself time to think about what I was going to say. "w-was o-okay..."

"Honey, you sound shaken up. Are you alright?" I heard a man's voice mumble something and shout, "Hey, princess! We need another round of shots over here!" My mom cursed. "Okay, I have to go; I'll be home at the normal time. I love you." And she hung up.

I felt bad for my mom having to be a bartender. I knew that wasn't her dream job. She was in school to be a journalist, working part-time at the bar to make some extra money. She and my dad had a plan: once I was born, she would stay home and focus on school and taking care of me, and my dad would be done with his firefighter training by then so he could be the provider for us.

Except, a month after I was born, there was an accident during a river rescue. The river was covered in ice; when my dad attempted to climb back on the surface after rescuing the victim, he got caught in a current and was swept away. His body was recovered two days later.

After that my mom didn't have a choice; she quit school and began working at the bar full-time. She said it wasn't too bad; there were lots of tips, and at least she had seniority to get the most shifts. My mom's friend Jessica would take care of me growing up, but she ended up getting a job at the hospital, so she became busy too, so I had a babysitter until I got to high school. Since then, I have gotten good at taking care of myself on the nights that my mom worked. Sometimes as I stared at the picture in the living room of my parents and me the day I was born, I would wonder how different life would be if my dad was alive. What memories I would have of him. What our house would look like. Maybe they could afford speech therapy for me... Maybe I wouldn't stutter anymore. But that was a life I would never know; my reality was much different.

I walked back to the bedroom and got changed into a pair of sweatpants and a t-shirt and got an icepack from the kitchen to put on my face. This wasn't anything new to me. The number of times I'd been beat up had been too many to keep track of. But each time my self-esteem had taken a hit. Luckily my mom was gone most days after school, so she typically wasn't around to see the damage. Sometimes on the days when she would be home, I would use her makeup to cover up my bruises so she wouldn't notice. I've gotten pretty good at using certain colours of foundation or concealer to cover up my bruises. I guess it helps that I have lots of experience with drawing and coloring my sketches.

Most nights after my homework was done, I would sit for hours and draw; mostly it would be random sketches that I would think of on a whim and create on the pages, but I have made a couple comic books. Not that I would ever publish them; there is no way they would be good enough to publish. But drawing was an outlet for me to forget the outside world and escape into whatever world that I had created. A world where pictures spoke louder than words. I could fully express myself without the embarrassment and frustration of stuttering. My mom always made sure we had enough pencils and sketchbooks for me to keep busy. She has always been supportive of my hobby; naïvely, she thinks I'll be famous one day. But I guess all mothers think that about their children.

After I iced my eye, I got into bed, put my hands together, and prayed.

> *Dear God, please help me find the strength I need to carry on. Thank you for everything you have blessed me with. But one last thing... I took a deep breath and closed my eyes. Please, please guide me in the way of some friends... I've been feeling really lonely lately... Thank you. Amen.*

CHAPTER TWO

RAY

I've thought about running away millions of times before. I had everything planned. I had a bag hidden in my closet that was pre-packed with clothes, food, and three passports tucked into one of the pockets. I was ready to go. Ready to escape. I sat in front of my bedroom window clutching the bag. All I would have to do was open it, grab the two of them, and run. Simple. I sat there for an hour. Sitting and waiting. Waiting for my mind to finally get enough courage. Ninety-nine percent of me was ready to throw myself out of that window and start a new life. But the remaining one percent is what always kept me from escaping. Ella and Daniel. What if we tried and got caught? What if we did run away but ended up on the streets...would that be safer? Possibly, but I couldn't be sure. With no money and no shelter, we wouldn't last long. I do work part-time at the boxing gym, but the pay isn't anything close to what we would need to keep the three of us fed, clothed, and sheltered someplace safe. I sat on the edge of my bed as I pondered possible places we could go to seek safety.

I heard footsteps coming towards my room. Initially I went into fight mode, but then my hearing picked up on who the footsteps belonged to, and my body immediately relaxed. Then the footsteps stopped, and my bedroom door slowly creaked open.

"Ray, what are you doing?" a soft, delicate voice asked.

"Ella, go to sleep. It's late." I ordered as I turned to look at her.

Her nose scrunched like it always did when she was upset. "Speak for yourself. Why do I have to go to bed when you get to stay up?" Her nightgown had stains from her toothpaste dried to it, and her dark curly hair was a mess, pointing in all directions. I smiled.

"Because I'm older than you. When you're seventeen, then you can stay up late too."

"But it's not fair! I'm only six and a half!" Her voice raised up an octave, and she jumped on my bed. "If you want me to sleep, then you have to let me sleep with you! "Deal?" She stuck her tiny hand out, and I shook it. "Deal."

She climbed on the opposite side of the bed, and then I adjusted the covers around her.

We lay next to each other in silence for a bit. The sound of her steady breathing calmed my nerves.

Just as I closed my eyes, she began to speak.

"Ray...do you think he will get better? When he isn't drinking, he can actually be really nice. And Daddy..."

Heat consumed my body. Before I could stop myself, my mouth opened.

"Don't ever call him that!" I roared.

I snapped. I didn't mean to. I was usually very careful around her. But my temper and I were constantly battling. It usually won.

She didn't seem fazed by my anger. Yelling was something we were both used to after years of living with that monster. "But he is our daddy, Ray. Even if he gets angry sometimes. Mommy said he wasn't always like this. Maybe he can change back?"

"Maybe," I muttered bitterly. "Now go to sleep."

"Goodnight," she whispered. I watched as her eyelids dropped as she let out a faint yawn.

I thought about what she said. *Maybe he can change back.*

It was a silly and naïve thing to say. Clearly, there was no way he could *change*. People like him were born monsters. Thriving off the pain and terror of others. I glanced at her delicate skin and the bruises along her body. I had some as well, but due to my size and age, I had the advantage of being able to fight back whenever *he* attacked me. Unfortunately for Ella, she wasn't so lucky.

We should have left years ago. If only my mom wasn't such an idiot. Why did she marry him anyway? Couldn't she see what an asshole he is? Why didn't she run away with us when we were kids? I'll never understand.

Flashes of anger shot through my body as I thought about him. How like tonight he'd go out with his friends to drink and then come home and treat us like shit. Memories of his threats and the pain of his beatings made me shake. My mind flashed to how quickly I snapped at Ella. How fast I was to react with anger. My worst fear haunted me daily.

You're turning into him. My brain teased. You're just like your father. Look at how fast you yelled at Ella. I could feel my body trying to protest the accusation; my hands were shaking, my heart was pounding, and my head was throbbing. Of course, I'm not like him; I would never be like him. I'm just stressed out, I tell myself. But the thoughts were racing through my mind faster than I could talk myself down.

It was too much for me to bear. I felt my body jolt up as I gasped for air. I didn't realize how much noise I had made until Ella practically jumped out of the bed.

"Are you okay, Ray? What happened?" she asked.

I was shaking. My heart was pounding. I tried my best to stay calm. "Nothing, just a bad dream, that's all."

She hugged me. "It's okay. We all have nightmares. I do too. Just close your eyes and go back to sleep, okay?"

I chuckled. "Isn't the older sibling supposed to be the brave one?"

Her eyes focused on mine as she spoke. "Sometimes even the bravest people get scared."

CHAPTER THREE

SAM

"Remember, you need to get to class on time because it's your first day, and first impressions are extremely important, especially for your father, and you need to be nice and talk to everyone, and you need to find your locker and…"

"I know! Geez, it's not my first day of high school; I'm in grade eleven, remember?" I blurted out.

My mom rolled her eyes. "I'm just making sure you're prepared because starting a new school isn't easy, especially as the new principal's daughter during second semester. Hopefully everything goes smoothly. I'm sure the people here are nice…"

My parents and I moved from New York City a week ago. It was an unexpected decision considering that both my parents and I have grown up there and that's where all of our family and friends live. Moving from the city to a quiet suburban area was going to take some time to get used to, but my dad got a promotion as the new principal at this school. He told us how he had hopes to turn the reputation around and increase the enrollment numbers; looking at the school, I wasn't so sure. It certainly wasn't as fancy-looking or clean as my old school. Most of the kids seemed indifferent or pissed off. At my old school, everyone at least smiled or waved at each other as they walked in. I noticed this group of three boys that gave me an unsettling feeling in my stomach. Something about them seemed dangerous. Living in a big city had made me hyper aware of sketchy people, especially being a young Black girl. You never knew what danger could be lurking around the corners. My parents always taught me to be aware of my surroundings; you could never be too careful.

My mom flashed me a mischievous smile as she noticed me looking at the three boys. "And who knows, maybe you'll meet a cute guy..."

I began to drift off to avoid listening to her lecture. She had always encouraged me to talk to boys in my class since I started high school. Each semester she'd ask me if I had any crushes on any of my classmates. The thing is, I did have a few crushes...

Just not on any of the boys.

I knew something about me was different since I was a kid. Whenever my mom would ask me if I had any crushes on the boys at school, I couldn't think of any that I found remotely attractive. Instead, a bunch of female classmates filled my mind. I was around the age of twelve when I knew for sure that I liked girls. I vowed to myself that I would keep it a secret.

Maybe one day I would be confident enough to tell my parents. But not today. I quickly said goodbye to my mom and stepped out of the car. I walked past the creepy-looking boys, who proceeded to wink at me and whistle. *Gross.* As I entered the hallway, I opened up the schedule that my dad printed off for me last night. I thought about visiting him in his new office, but knowing how stressed out he was last night and how he left for work at 6:30am despite school starting at 8:30am, I decided against it. I'd just visit him on my lunch.

My eyes scanned the schedule as I searched for my homeroom class.

English. Room 334.

I made my way up the crowded staircases filled with students staring at me with wonder. I heard endless whispers that carried across the halls.

"Who is she?"

"Is she new?"

"Has she always been here?"

I tried to ignore them and keep moving. Usually, I wasn't shy, but starting over in an entirely new school was a bit nerve-wracking for me. I moved past the groups of people chatting on the staircase and entered the third floor.

Blocking my way was a large circle of students gathered in the middle of the hallway. Some were cheering, others had their phones out and were recording something. When I got closer, I noticed what everyone was fussing about. In the middle of the circle were the three mean-looking boys I noticed outside the school. There was the shortest one, who had a bulldog tattoo on his upper arm, who stood back, clapping. Then there was a redhead boy who was holding someone's legs as they were sprawled on the ground. Then the tallest of the trio opened his mouth and spat at the person on the ground. I had to peek under someone's arm to get a good look at the boy on the ground. He was smaller than the boys that were taunting him. I noticed a bruise around his right eye. My stomach immediately turned in disgust and rage.

"Hey Stutter Boy! Are you going to talk normally today, or are you still learning your ABCs from Elmo, you freak?" the tallest boy teased.

I looked at the boy and noticed that he was about to cry. His hands were shaking in fear. Anger boiled inside of me. This was *wrong*.

The redhead laughed as he spoke, "I think he's about to cry. "Hey, stutter boy, are you about to cry?"

The one with the tattoo snuck up behind the boy as his friend was talking and yanked the top of his boxers. The boy yelped in protest, and the crowd roared with laughter.

Without thinking, I pushed my way into the middle of the circle in front of the boy.

People instantly went quiet as they waited for the drama to continue.

The leader smirked at me, "What do you think you're doing?"

I stood up straighter and looked him right in the eyes as I replied. "Stopping you and your friends from hurting this poor guy, what did he even do to you anyway?"

A wave of snickers penetrated the confined area. The three bullies burst into laughter.

"Who are you? Do you think you're some sort of superhero or something? You should know that since you are a girl, that means you're too weak to even do anything." The redhead exclaimed.

I could feel my body heat up. Before I knew what I was doing, my foot soared right into his private area. He hunched over in pain, and his friends and the kids watching broke into laughter.

"Woah, bro! She got you good." The bulldog tattoo boy snickered.

Instantly the boy stumbled away but not before flipping me off and giving the boy on the floor a wicked glare. His friends followed him, and the crowd went off in various directions, laughing and gossiping as they would occasionally turn back to glance at me. Eventually it was just the boy, and I left.

"T-thank you-u." he spat out.

"You don't need to thank me. Those jerks got what they deserved. My name's Samantha, but everyone calls me Sam. What about you?"

The boy shyly answered, "E-Ethan. Sorry for st-uttering-g I c-can't h-help it-t."

"Don't apologize! Are you okay?' I asked.

Ethan nodded though he didn't seem too confident. "Yeah, I'm uu-used to it. ."

I pointed to his black eye. "Did they do that to you too?"

Ethan's cheeks flushed as he replied, "A couple days ago, but it's okay; it's not t-too bad."

I was surprised no teacher stepped in. I looked around, and all of the classroom doors were shut. I knew that the school had a bad reputation. But how would teachers let this stuff happen? I was lost in thought when I heard the bell ring.

"Oh, shoot! I'm late to class; it's my first day here. Do you know where I can find room English in room 334?"

He nodded and gestured for me to follow him. When we arrived at my classroom, Ethan entered with me.

"Looks like we're in the same class; that's cool," I noted. Ethan smiled, and we walked in together.

The teacher seemed nice, a classic English teacher. Wool cardigan, glasses, and writing on the chalkboard. I read what she was writing; *why were the curtains blue?*

Oh boy. I knew immediately this would be the class where we needed to analyze every detail in the books even when the author didn't even intend for it to be intentional. Welcome to High School English.

When the teacher finished writing, she turned and noticed me. "Hello! Welcome, you must be Samantha Myers, Principal Myers' daughter!"

I could feel the heart rush to my cheeks. Not that I wanted it to be a secret that my dad was the new principal, but it being the first thing people found out about me was probably social suicide. Who would want to be friends with the principal's daughter? I mustered up a smile and nodded as I looked around at my classmates, who were either uninterested or had already started to zone her out and had no idea what she had said.

"My name is Mrs. Simon. You can sit here next to Raymond; the desk next to his is an extra." She gestured to the back row where a boy was sitting who I assumed was Raymond.

I put my backpack down beside my desk and took a seat. As Mrs. Simon continued to write on the chalkboard, I glanced at Raymond, who was ripping off the corner of his notebook. Clearly, he wasn't very interested in the lesson. I looked over to Ethan, who was sitting beside a girl who was anxiously writing down every word Mrs. Simon was writing. Ethan noticed me looking at him, and he smiled as he took out his book to write too. I guess I should do the same, but considering there was no notebook on my desk, I decided to just listen for today. I'd ask Mrs. Simon for a notebook later.

Raymond turned to me unexpectedly. "Sorry, I zoned out for a bit. But you can't blame me; this is the second time we have talked about the curtains this week," he rolled his eyes, "also, call me Ray, not Raymond."

I chuckled, "Yeah, my old English teacher talked about the significance of blueberry pie in a month; I get it." Ray smirked. "I go by Sam, not Samantha, by the way," I added. Ray nodded and then continued to rip away at his notebook.

I half listened until the period had ended. From what I had gathered, the curtains were blue to signify some guy being depressed? Mrs. Simon began to talk about what other colours of curtains in the book could mean, but she was cut off by the bell.

Ray picked up his backpack and headed down the hallway without saying goodbye; Ethan waited for me at the doorway.

"D-do you need help fin-finding your next c-class?" he asked. I glanced at my schedule; I had geography in room 214. I showed Ethan, and he gestured for me to follow him. I noticed Ray begin to walk into a classroom labelled Resource Room. Ethan noticed me looking. "That is the su-suportt room. Ray is in grade tw-twelve, b-but he takes grade eleven eng-lish wwwith us." He explained.

I guess Ray isn't a fan of English, but I don't blame him; I'm not either. Although, there is no way I could afford to fail a grade if I wanted to get my Ph.D. in Marine Biology, which has been my dream for as long as I can remember. I had always worked hard to maintain my A+ average. Growing up, my dad always instilled the idea that each grade level was preparation for higher education, and if that was my goal, I needed to take each level seriously and not develop any bad habits. I guess that's the educator in him talking, but he wasn't wrong. I felt bad for Ray; hopefully, the extra support would set him up to be on track for next year. I couldn't imagine how stressed out that must be making him.

Ethan pointed out my next two classrooms and the cafeteria on the way to my next period. I had English, geography, lunch, science, and gym. Not too bad. Ethan and I made a plan to meet at the cafeteria for lunch since we had the same lunch break. I was very happy about that; he was the only friend I had made so far, and I didn't want to eat alone. As I walked into my next class, I got ready to be introduced to the classroom again as the principal's daughter... Lucky me.

CHAPTER FOUR

ETHAN

I watched as Mrs. Darbus drew a sloppy triangle on the board. She wasn't much of an artist. The lines weren't straight at all, and it looked more like a square than a triangle. As she finished, she rubbed her hands together in an attempt to wipe off the chalk and turned towards the class. "Who can tell me the name of this triangle?"

I squinted at the board and tried to make out the mess of squiggly lines. I noticed that one line was longer than the other and guessed it was a scalene triangle. I watched as the rest of the class stared at the board, clearly bewildered, and asked their friends for the answer. I must admit that their cluelessness amused me. Mrs. Darbus looked around the room with disgust and shame. As soon as she looked in my direction, I struggled not to make eye contact. Most kids are uncomfortable with being asked to speak aloud in class, but my stuttering makes everything I do ten times more nerve-racking. I *hate* when teachers make me speak in front of the class or do oral presentations. It's just another chance to get laughed at. My teachers usually understand that and try their best to minimize my pain and embarrassment, but Mrs. Darbus either doesn't care or is oblivious to how it will affect me.

Her eyes settled on me, and a grin spread across her face. "Ethan, why don't you tell me the answer?"

Instantly everyone in the room was staring at me. Their heavy gazes pierced through my brain. My heart began to flutter uncontrollably, and my throat was closing up, making it nearly impossible to speak.

"I only need one word from you, my dear; don't overreact." She stated.

I took a deep breath and noticed a few people whispering. I tried my best to clear my mind and focus on what I wanted to say. *Scalene.* That's all I had to say.

"S-Sca—" My voice paused before continuing the word, "—lene."

I wanted to turn invisible. As soon as I sputtered out the answer, the classroom erupted. Some people had their heads back as laughter escaped their lips, while others sneakily snickered amongst their friends. Mrs. Darbus tried to tell everyone to keep quiet, but her attempts were drowned out by the dull roar.

I wanted to disappear. Turn invisible. Escape.

It felt like the entire world was mocking me. I couldn't stop it. So many people were laughing and pointing at me. Billy Sampson even fell out of his chair from laughing so hard. I was about to run out of the classroom when I was saved.

The bell rang.

I packed my bag in a hurry and rushed out of the room, bumping into people as I ran past them. I could feel the tears streaming down my face. My body felt cold and numb. I wanted to get home; I wanted to escape. As I turned the corner, my face smacked into something hard.

A taunting voice bellowed above me, "What the—
"

As I looked up, I recognized *him.* It was Brock.

When we made eye contact, he shot me a vicious smile. "Hey, what's up, Stutter Boy?" He wrapped his arms around me in a slight chokehold. His dark eyes gleamed with joy as he guided me along the hallway.

I tried my best to stay calm. I didn't want him to see my fear.

I saw Sam at her locker. I had only known her for less than a day, but she was the closest thing I had to a friend. Seeing her gave me a sense of comfort. I prayed that she'd see me. She dug a textbook out of her bag and turned her head. *She saw me.* I noticed her eyes become filled with anger as she glared at Brock.

Brock noticed her too and waved. "Isn't that your little friend? How cute. I didn't know you had any friends, Stutter Boy."

I noticed the girl's washroom coming up. Before I could register what was happening, my body was shoved forward. I tried to break my fall, but I landed face-first onto the hard ceramic tile. *Splat!* My face burned from both pain and embarrassment. I could hear Brock's obnoxious laughter trailing down the hall.

I felt something touch my shoulder. As I turned, I saw a girl staring at me. She looked young, probably a freshman. Her eyes studied me carefully.

"Are you okay…you do realize this is the girl's washroom, right?" the girl asked. Her voice was laced with a mixture of worry and sarcasm.

I quickly stumbled to my feet and nodded. I was in no mood to talk and make a bigger fool of myself.

She snickered and looked like she was about to say something else, but Sam barged into the washroom, grabbed my hand, and pulled me back into the hallway.

"Ethan! Are you alright?" Sam asked as she took a deep breath to calm herself down. "That guy is such an idiot! How do people feel joy from terrorizing others?" Her flushed face contrasted against her dark skin. Her hands were in fists at her side; for a second, I was worried the washroom door was about to get punched.

"I'm okay," I muttered. From the corner of my eye, I noticed Ray Martinez looking at us from his locker. We went to elementary school together. My mom used to tell me that his mom and my mom were close in high school. Apparently after his mom graduated, she got married to this older guy, and our moms eventually lost track of each other. Ray never bullied me or anything, so by that standard he was considered one of the nice kids in school. He was quiet like me; I would notice him say a few words to people here and there, but I never saw him hanging out with any friends during recess or lunch breaks. I guess we had that in common. I wondered if he saw everything that had happened. He must have. When we locked eyes, he quickly turned and walked towards the exit door. I don't blame him. If I was him, I wouldn't want to get involved either. I really don't get why Sam cares so much. But I'm grateful for it.

Sam seemed to be calmer as we walked down the hallway together. "Do you want to walk home together? I live two blocks over." I nodded. Her house is in the richer area, of course; I overheard that her dad is the new principal. Maybe that's why she cares so much, trying to make a good first impression? Or maybe she is desperate for someone to hang out with. She will probably move on once she meets new people. A girl like her, brave, pretty, and smart, won't have a hard time making friends at all. For now, I will enjoy her company. As we walked along the sidewalk, I couldn't help but smile. For once, I didn't feel so alone.

CHAPTER FIVE

RAY

One. Two. Three. *BOOM!*

One. Two. Three. *BOOM!*

One. Two. Three. *BOOM!*

The sound of my fist connecting against the punching bag echoed throughout the gym. I practiced at the boxing gym every day after school for hours straight. It was a good distraction from all the shit going on at home. I always made sure to be home before *he* got home though. I tried my best to shelter Daniel and Ella from the violence. Though they were both old enough to understand now, even Ella. Nights always ended the same way. Screaming, crying, and crashing plates. Eventually…with punches flying.

The boxing gym was small but a decent enough size for people to train. There were a couple of older guys outside talking as they lit up cigars. I wasn't alone inside; there was another guy practicing his kicks with a guy who I assume was his trainer. He must be rich to afford one of those. All the guys that come in here are middle-aged men having midlife crises or old guys coming to smoke cigars and have locker room talk before they go home to their wives and kids. Today was a slow day, and my manager was off, so I took advantage and did some training too. Once the other guy and his trainer packed up and left, it was time to close it up. I took a sip out of my water bottle, picked up my backpack from my locker, and headed home. The boxing gym isn't too far from my house, which is good, especially for times when I need to get home quickly. The manager is very relaxed, so he doesn't mind if I need to leave in a hurry. Plus, it isn't usually busy; I think it may even be closing down soon, but I hope not. I liked the place.

I checked the time on my phone, 5:24pm, no texts. Usually, Daniel will update me if any emergencies happen, like Mom burning the food that she was preparing for dinner, which happens a lot. Her anxiety about *him* not enjoying dinner often leads to her overcooking her dish or leaving it unattended as she juggles her other tasks. In that case I usually stop by the supermarket and get food from the hot table. Luckily, *he* is always too drunk to notice that the meals weren't homemade. I shudder at the thought of what would happen if *he* ever found out. Daniel would also text me if there was ever a time when that monster would come home early. Most of the time he hangs out at the local bar until he is kicked out and sent home by the bartender— Ethan Suzuki's mom. I thought about today at school. Poor Ethan. Watching him get pushed into the girl's washroom was rough. I wished that I had done something. But in the moment, I froze. My survival instincts kicked in; I had enough violence at home. Do I really need it at school too? The voice in my head spoke up again: Are *you sure it's your 'survival instincts,' or are you just a coward like him? Maybe you don't care seeing people get hurt because deep down you like it. It must be in your blood.* I shook my head in an attempt to make the thoughts disappear. I know they aren't true, but I do feel guilty. I should have done something. And I didn't.

I try my best to be invisible. From my classmates and mainly the teachers. If any of the teachers noticed my bruises, they would ask me questions. If they asked me questions or just simply suspected something even without questioning me about it, they would then be obligated to contact Children's Aid. That would be a nightmare. I was also worried about making friends and having them get too close. What if they asked to hang out at my house? Or they start to notice how jittery I am when it comes to talking about my home life. It's better to stay neutral and have casual conversation but not too often, where becoming friends is an option. It's better to be safe. I can't risk something getting out to people at school or their parents. If it does, it could be bad. While I do want that monster to go to jail and pay for what he has done, I worry about my siblings. I'm not eighteen yet; I can't get custody. If they split us up, that would kill me. I can't let that happen. My mom wouldn't be much help. In my opinion, she should go to jail too. For staying with him, for watching as we get abused, and for doing nothing. Daniel doesn't agree. He is more empathetic than I am. He thinks Mom is just scared and is trying to protect us as best as she can. But he is too young, too young to remember the nights I spent crying to her, begging her to take us away before Ella was even born. Mom would just turn stone cold, no expression, and then walk away. As if she was frozen over. After a few years I stopped begging. Then she got pregnant with Ella. Daniel was four; I was ten. That's when I begged her again. She had to leave now. She couldn't bring another baby into this mess. But she did. And I learned to stop turning to her for help. She didn't care. Or she was too scared to care. Either way, my siblings needed someone to protect them. It wasn't her. So, then it had to be me.

When I was fourteen, I started collecting supplies in a getaway bag, which was just my old backpack that is full of holes and faulty zippers, but it's better than nothing. I stole our passports from the box in the basement one night while everyone was sleeping and the monster was passed out on the couch with a half-empty beer in his hand. Over time I had collected old clothing of ours that didn't fit perfectly anymore but could work if needed temporarily. For food and water, I had taken some plastic water bottles, a few cans of beans, some candy, and canned meat. Not exactly five-star meal material, but enough to keep us alive until we could find somewhere safe to stay. All I needed was the perfect plan and timing to execute our escape. It had to be perfect, or else the consequences would be too dangerous...maybe even deadly. Most kids my age are talking about where they are applying to college and which programs they want to get into. I could never afford college. Though I could get a grant or a loan, it still isn't in the cards for me. Education wasn't my main goal; I can't even consider that until I get my siblings and me away from this nightmare. Maybe someday, but certainly not until we are safe and stable enough for me to be able to leave.

As soon as I walked onto my street, my heart began to race. My eyes were locked onto the red pickup truck on the driveway. *Fuck.* I scanned my phone for texts from Daniel, thinking I may have missed something, but there was nothing there. Which means he came home unexpectedly and was angry. I ran up to the front door, fumbled in my pocket for my keys...

And then I heard screaming.

CHAPTER SIX

SAM

"So, how have your first two weeks been at the new school?" Mom asked as she put the platter of chicken and potatoes on the table.

I shrugged. "It's been good; I made a new friend. His name is Ethan." As soon as I said it, I immediately regretted it. I realized where her mind would go.

I could see the smile forming on my mom's face as she nudged my dad with her elbow. My mom was desperate for me to find love. She and my dad met when they were in high school. They've been together as long as they can remember. And as long as I could remember, my mom has been telling me their love story; they met when they both had the same gym period. My dad got confused on the first day and walked into the girl's changeroom. My mom laughed at him, and my dad was obviously very embarrassed; luckily, my mom was the only one there at the time. After that they started to chat after gym class as they walked to their next period together, and the rest was history. My mom always hoped that I would meet my match in high school as well. I mean, I wouldn't mind falling in love, except that would look different than how my parents are picturing it to be.

My dad rolled his eyes at her playfully. "Leave her alone; she can make friends without everything being romantic." He smiled at me and continued, "How did you and Ethan meet? Do you have a class together?"

"Yes, we have English class together, but we met on my first day in the morning. I was making my way to my classroom when I saw him getting beaten up by some idiots, so I stepped in," I replied.

My dad's expression turned from happy to disgust within seconds. "What!? I never heard about this. Didn't any teachers get involved? Nobody thought to inform me?" His voice got louder and louder as he spoke. I guess I get my sense of justice from him, the need to help others. I debated telling them more details, but then my mom asked, "That's horrible; how did you step in? Did you get a teacher? ."

No, I kicked him between his legs. I thought. My dad studied my expression; he could always read me well. He could tell I did something more than what my mom suggested.

"Samantha...what happened?" he asked accusingly.

I guess there's no turning back now. "Well, no teachers were around. Ethan told me that most teachers ignore school fights because the previous principal told them to not get involved. So, I told them to leave him alone. Then one of them said that since I'm a girl, I wouldn't be able to stop them anyway... so..." my voice trailed off. My mom was gripping onto her water glass for dear life. Terrified of what I was about to say next. My dad's eyebrow was raised up so high it was almost attached to the top of his buzzcut. He nodded for me to continue. So, I did. "Then I kicked him in the private area..." my mom gasped, and my dad looked at me for a second before starting to laugh.

Definitely not an expected reaction. But I'll take it.

"Damian! That is not funny! You should not be encouraging violence, especially as the school principal," my mom scolded.

My dad shrugged, "Yes, sweetheart, but at the same time I'm proud of her. If those boys were seriously injuring Ethan and no teacher was brave enough to stand up for him, then I am glad our girl did." He winked at me.

My mom shook her head and started to anxiously clean up the dinner table as she typically does when she is upset about something.

My dad's expression became more serious as he leaned closer to me. "I am going to address this at the staff meeting tomorrow. I will not tolerate this behavior from staff or students. I will make it known that any form of bullying will lead to suspension or expulsion if necessary. Also, if any staff member refuses to get involved in instances of bullying or threats, they will receive consequences."

I knew my dad was serious. He always told me to stand up to bullies, and as a teacher at his old school, he would often check in with all of his students to make sure the classroom environment was safe and welcoming. I know my parents are good people. I know they are kind, loving, and accepting. But still, everyone has limits, right?

Boundaries of where the acceptance stops and judgement begins. I just don't know where theirs are. And I'm too afraid to find out. After we cleaned up the kitchen, I went upstairs to finish up my homework.

As I entered my room, I noticed laughter coming from outside. I peeked through my bedroom window and noticed a girl that I recognized from school. She was entering the house next door; her cellphone was wedged between her neck and shoulder as she carried a shopping bag into the house. It looked like a bag from the bookstore nearby. I could feel my stomach tighten. Who *was making her laugh? Maybe she had a boyfriend.* I wouldn't be surprised; a girl as beautiful as her certainly had a boyfriend. I tried to snap myself out of my jealous thoughts. I admit I had a little crush on her but not enough to know if I really liked her. I still didn't even know her name. I had thought to ask Ethan, but I didn't want him to suspect anything. You can't fall in love with someone you don't even really know, right? We didn't even have any classes together, but I have seen her in the hallways often, and whenever we crossed paths, I could instantly feel the heat rush to my cheeks and couldn't help but hold my breath. It didn't matter anyway. It's not like I could ever actually talk to her. Or if I did, I could never hint at my feelings. There was no way she would like me back. She would probably think I was a freak. I pulled myself away from the window and turned my attention to Gary, my turtle. He was probably hungry.

"Hi Gary!" I say as I feed him his favorite food, mealworms. My mom could never watch me feed him;

she finds it too gross. I find it fascinating. I dreamed of having more pets like axolotls or some saltwater creatures, but my mom hardly let me have Gary. My dad had to convince her, and eventually she agreed to gift me Gary on my tenth birthday. Someday, when I have my own home, I imagine it will be full of different tanks and marine life. I couldn't wait.

Gary was constantly hiding from the moment I got him. He only came out to eat and when I would clean his tank. But I guess I can't judge him, because in a way I'm constantly hiding as well…

****

"T-thank you for p-picking m-me up every m-morning," Ethan said as we walked to school.

I waved my hand nonchalantly as I replied, "No big deal, I don't mind."

Since my first day of school, Ethan and I had come up with a system. I would walk to his house, and then we would walk to school together. Even though I live closer to school, we agreed that it would be safer since his bullies usually find a way to corner him on his way to school and home. Since I've been walking with him, they have left us alone minus some light insults and snickering. I think my dad's staff meeting also helped. The teachers now always had their classroom doors open and even took turns monitoring the hallways. It is definitely much harder for them to hurt Ethan now with the extra eyes around. Ethan felt more comfortable too, I could tell; he wasn't constantly looking around and walking at lightspeed down the sidewalk like when I first met him. His body was more relaxed and less tense. I was glad. Ethan was a good friend; I hated seeing how antsy and on edge he always was. Since I started the new school, Ethan was the only friend I had made so far, but I was content with that. Ethan didn't like talking to new people, he worried they would judge his stuttering. Plus, I was always more inclined to have one or two close friends rather than a large group. Most large friend groups turn out to be full of drama anyway, and I had no desire for New York high school girl drama.

We walked by a house with a red pickup truck in the driveway. I could hear noises coming from inside, almost like someone was yelling or throwing stuff, or both. Ethan looked over and winced. "T-that's Ray's h-house," he whispered.

"Ray? From English class?" I asked. Ethan nodded.

Whatever was going on didn't look good, but I didn't want to judge. I know that parents fight. Mine have a few times, though not that loudly and not that violently. But maybe it wasn't as bad as it sounds.

Maybe I was just imagining the sound of broken glass.

The door swung open, and I saw Ray. He looked tired, almost like he didn't sleep. Though thinking about it, he always looked tired. His head was down, but his lips were in a tight line, and his hands were clutching the straps of his backpack so tightly that his knuckles were white. He was walking so fast that he almost bumped into me.

"Hey, watch out!" I warned.

Ray's head snapped up; clearly, he was so lost in thought he didn't even realize we were there. Instantly his eyes widened as his head turned back to look at his house. Almost like he was trying to judge if we were close enough to hear the commotion going on inside. He opened his mouth to say something, but before he could speak, the door swung open again. This time it was a man walking out who I assumed was his dad. He had a cigarette in one hand and a bottle in the other. It looked like a beer bottle, but I doubted it actually was. He wouldn't be driving drunk...would he? The man looked mean and miserable. He was muttering curse words under his breath as he got into his truck. Ray looked mortified. As if we had just witnessed something we weren't supposed to. I wanted to apologize, though I wasn't sure what to apologize for. We didn't mean to walk by while his parents were in a fight. As the truck was catching up to us, I noticed the passenger window rolling down.

Ray noticed something and yelled, "Duck down!"

Ethan and I did. Before I could ask why, the bottle that his dad was holding when he got into the car flew out of the window and shattered onto the ground beside us. His dad yelled something incoherent as he passed by us and then drove off.

I took another look at the bottle and recognized the logo from my dad's garage fridge.

It was a beer bottle.

He just threw a beer bottle at us.

Ray looked mortified.

He quickly muttered an apology under his breath and began to run ahead of us. He was a fast runner. I wanted to try to catch up to him and ask him if he was okay, but I decided to let him go. He clearly didn't want to talk about what just happened.

Ethan looked at me and then looked at the bottle. We both then continued to walk to school without saying a word. Though I knew we were both thinking the same thing, Ray was clearly in some sort of trouble.

But what should we do?

CHAPTER SEVEN

ETHAN

I could hardly keep my eyes away from Ray. I tried my best not to stare, but my mind was still replaying the events from this morning. The shouting. The sound of broken glass. The beer bottle. The look on Ray's face before he ran away. I didn't blame him; I would have probably run away too. Sam and I haven't spoken since; our entire walk to school was in heavy silence. I could tell Sam wasn't sure how to act around Ray, especially since they sit next to each other. Ray was focused on the board ahead as Mrs. Simon was writing. This is the most that I have noticed him paying attention in class all year. Though I doubt he is even hearing a word Mrs. Simon is saying. Neither am I. It isn't until a paper is placed on my desk that I snap my gaze away from Ray. I read it, Group Assignment, Short Story. Then, the column below, Group Members: Ethan Suzuki, Samantha Myers, Raymond Martinez.

Well, this is awkward.

I catch Sam shooting me a look from her desk; I can't tell if she is happy to be with Ray or worried. Maybe she is still figuring that out herself. Ray, however, looks like he would rather disintegrate into the floorboards and never be seen again. I wonder if he is going to drop out of the class, but I remember that he is already doing a catch-up course, and if he fails again, there is no way he can apply for colleges. I feel bad for him; it must be hard to do homework with whatever is happening at his house. Up until Sam started hanging around, I struggled with it too. I tried my best to do all my homework and study, but some nights, especially after running into Brock and his crew of idiots. I couldn't find the energy to do any work at all.

The bell rang, and everybody got up. I noticed Ray was the first to exit the room. Sam looked like she was about to say something to him, but clearly, he wasn't ready to talk to us. Sam looked at me and said the first thing she has said to me all morning.

"This will be an interesting assignment."

****

I waited for Sam in the hallway as she was in the washroom. We planned on brainstorming ideas for our short story on our walk home. Maybe if we have a few ideas in mind, we could use them as a conversation starter tomorrow with Ray. I tried to think of some ideas. A lost dog? Superheroes? Evil Santa Claus?

My thoughts were interrupted by my body being slammed into a locker.

I haven't been in this situation for a while. Apparently, Sam's dad made new rules, so the teachers have to patrol the hallways during school hours to make sure nobody is getting into trouble. But unfortunately for me, school ended ten minutes ago. I looked around and didn't see any teachers; the doors to the classroom around us were shut. I guess most teachers didn't like the idea of volunteering their time to monitor the hallways after school. Great.

"Hey stu-tt-er boy!" Brock mocked.

I rolled my eyes. Here we go again.

Brock balled his hand into a fist; I braced for the impact. Before he could punch me, I felt his grip loosen on me, and I heard a body being thrown on the floor.

It wasn't me. It was Brock.

Standing over him was Ray. Brock looked terrified. I couldn't help but smile at the sight.

"Would you quit being a jerk and leave him alone! If I see you bothering him or anyone else again, you'll regret it!" Ray yelled.

Ray was shorter than Brock but stronger. I knew he worked at the boxing gym; he must be training there too; he was much more muscular than Brock.

I waited for something to happen. For Brock to stand up and punch him. Or his friends to come to his rescue. Instead, I noticed his friends slowly backing away until they ran out the exit door. What cowards.

Brock stood up and looked around, noticing his friends were gone. He looked at Ray, and I waited for a reaction. Instead, Brock just ran out the exit door without saying a word. No snarky remark. No threats. He was just gone.

Then I noticed Sam standing behind me. She looked just as shocked as I was. We looked at Ray, and then suddenly the three of us burst out into harmonious laughter.

"That was amazing, Ray!" Sam exclaimed.

Ray chuckled, "No, not really; he was just super light. All bark and no fight… I'm sorry I never said anything before. Maybe I should've." He turned to look at me, and I shook my head.

"N-no, i-t's o-okay," I said.

We walked down the hallway together towards the exit door. I could tell Sam and I were thinking the same thing. *Should we mention it this morning?*

As if he could read my mind, Ray stopped once we got to the sidewalk, and his face turned serious.

"You have to promise me that you won't say anything about this morning. Also, don't walk by my house anymore. Take the street on the other side; I mean it. I know we are going to have to talk because of the English assignment, but that's it. We aren't friends. No personal life talk, okay?"

Sam and I looked at each other. I know Sam; she would want to help. Maybe tell her dad, but she also would want to respect his privacy. At least until we knew more information.

"We promise, right, Ethan?" Sam asked. I nodded. Ray gave us a head nod.

Before he could start walking down the other path, I asked, "W-w-would you want to m-meet at my place tomorrow to w-work on it?"

Sam agreed, and Ray took a second to think it over before agreeing as well. We planned to meet tomorrow after school to brainstorm different story ideas.

Sam and I walked down the other street like we had promised Ray. As we walked, I couldn't help but have a bad feeling in my stomach. Like us not doing anything wasn't a good idea. It was too late now, though; at least Ray is starting to trust us. I didn't want to ruin that.

I just hoped for his sake that his dad wasn't home when he arrived.

CHAPTER EIGHT

RAY

When he isn't home, things could actually seem normal about our lives. My mom was in the kitchen preparing lasagna for dinner; her apron had tomato sauce stains on it, and her hair was wrapped up in a messy bun. She had the radio on; she was singing along to some old Bon Jovi song. She looked happy. Looking at her like this, you could pass off that she was this joyful housewife with a loving husband and three happy-go-lucky kids. That is until you get a glimpse of the bruises covering her legs and arms. They show the horror behind the Hallmark wife effect she hides behind. It amazes me that nobody ever notices when she goes out. Though she only ever goes out to buy groceries, just once a week for thirty minutes, with his red pickup truck parked in the no-park zone. Waiting, monitoring, spying. She is timed carefully. One minute late. It's over. I remember one time as a kid when Daniel was still in a car seat; we were in the car waiting for Mom to finish her grocery shopping. He was staring at his watch anxiously, counting down minute by minute. I was too young to understand all of the horrific details, but I had witnessed enough to know that if Mommy didn't come home soon, she would be in trouble. And I didn't like watching her get in trouble. Unfortunately for my mom, the store was extra busy that day, and they were short-staffed. Thirty-one minutes had gone by. He cursed, ordered me to stay in the car with

Daniel, and marched into the store. My stomach sank. Mommy was going to be in trouble.

Of course, now I know why he was so worried. His fear is someone talking to her, or her talking to someone, exposing his abuse. Trying to break free. The thought made me scoff; I couldn't even imagine her trying. She was too dedicated to him. Too loyal or too scared, maybe both. Either way, I didn't buy either excuse. It was her job to save us. We are trapped in this house of horrors because of her. When I was younger and used to beg her to take us away and leave him, she would make excuses for him. Point out that he only gets angry because he has diabetes, that he is just afraid he is going to get sick and have to leave us alone, so he wants everything to be perfect while he is still here because he is afraid of dying young. Yeah, right. I don't get how she buys that ridiculous garbage he spews at her. His idea of wanting "everything to be perfect" means everyone needs to walk on eggshells around him. A missing beer in the fridge (even though he was the one who drank it), a spilled drop of milk while pouring him coffee, or the food being too spicy or not spicy enough in his mind are grounds for getting in trouble.

Usually, it is Mom that suffers the worst of it. I will step in at times, and then I become the bad guy. Daniel knows better; I've taught him to take Ella into a different room to hide until things calm down. He is better at avoiding conflict than facing it, which is good. I don't want him or Ella getting involved anyway. Though he would still hit them sometimes when I'm not home, but if he does, I make sure he pays for it. Mom will try to stop me, and we will end up fighting in the kitchen or the living room. Just like what happened when Sam and Ethan walked by that morning. I had woken up to screaming. He was yelling at Ella. She had wet the bed. Apparently, that was grounds for punishment. I wasn't going to let that happen. It bothers him now that I am old enough to fight back. He is still stronger than me, but we are almost the same height now, and I've gained some muscle since I've been working at the boxing gym. I know he has noticed, but it has just made him angrier and more determined to hit me even harder. After our fights, Mom would either try to comfort him or scold me and tell me to mind my own business. As if that is easy to do when every day feels like Hell. My mom always forgives him too easily, as if his blowups were as minor as someone spilling water on the tablecloth. Sometimes he comes home with flowers or jewelry, apologizes, she forgives him, and the cycle continues. It's like watching a rerun of the same movie again and again. The bad guy gets away with it every single time.

Ella and Daniel were watching an old episode of Hannah Montana on TV. Daniel doesn't actually like it; it's too girly for him, but he will watch it for her. He knows the only TV time we get is when he isn't home, so we let Ella take over the TV for as long as she wants. It's the least we could do to try to combat all of the pain she sees in her real life. I let myself relax on the couch for a second and pretend that this was my normal life. Happy mom making home-cooked meals, my younger siblings watching Disney Channel. Life is good. Life is easy. Life is safe.

Until the front door opens.

I snap back to reality, Daniel shuts the TV off, and my mom goes into performance mode. The radio is turned off, her messy apron is removed, and she smiles like those housewives from old TV shows.

"Hi, my love! How was your day? " she asks. I know what she is thinking. She is praying to heaven that he had a good day. As if he is the one with the hard life. All he does is work at his cousin's car shop, go to the bar for hours, come home, and beat up his wife. We are the ones overanalyzing every move we make in an attempt to please him.

He takes off his baseball cap and plants it on the kitchen table. It's perfectly set; the food is ready to serve. I couldn't think of anything that she had missed. But then his eyes glance over to the fridge.

Oh no. She forgot his beer.

Certainly, a man who just got kicked out of the bar isn't in dire need of more beer, right? Wrong. My mom is usually pretty good about this, but he came home early today. She wasn't ready. I shot Daniel a look, and he understood; he grabbed Ella's hand, and they quietly snuck into her bedroom down the hall and shut the door.

At first, he said nothing; my mom quickly went to the fridge and grabbed a beer out of it. Before she could reach the bottle opener, the beer was yanked out of her hand.

"Do you know how badly I needed this?!" he roared.

My mom's lips quivered. Here we go.

"Y-yes, my love. I am very sorry." She begged.

"The damn bar closed early today! Apparently, they are cutting the bartenders' hours because of budget cuts or some crap. Then I come home to my house! Where I expect the decency of being greeted by my wife with a damn beer in her hand! What do I get instead? A lousy pan of pasta!" He raised his hand; I thought he was going to hit her. Instead, the pasta dish went flying, the glass container shattering on the floor. The tomato sauce and pasta noodles painted the walls.

My mom whimpered, and he stepped closer to her.

That's when my hands landed around his neck.

My mom screamed. He threw the beer bottle at my chest. It hurt, but I don't think it cut me through my shirt, but it was enough to startle me and loosen my grip on him. Then he slammed me into the countertop. He is going to kill me. Before he could continue, my mom began to cry and beg him to leave me alone and punish her instead.

"Clean this mess up before I come back, and you better have something for me to eat." He responded. Then he slapped her across the face, grabbed another beer out of the fridge, slammed the backyard door closed, and sat on the lawn chair outside as he cracked the beer open.

I got lucky. I guess he wanted a beer more than he wanted to kill me tonight.

CHAPTER NINE

SAM

It's been a month since we handed in our English assignment, yet we still find ourselves hanging out at Ethan's house every day after school. Ray comes most days except when he has a shift at the boxing gym, which is about twice a week. Even though he said we weren't going to be friends after the assignment was done, it looks like he changed his mind. We still haven't mentioned anything about that morning with his dad, and I don't think he wants us to. There isn't much for him to say anyway; Ethan and I have a good idea of what is happening. It's hard not to notice the days when Ray has a cut on his lip or a bruise on his leg. I've thought about mentioning something to my dad, but I knew that would upset Ray. I don't want to lose him as a friend; it seems like Ethan and I are the only two people in the world that he has to turn to. Though Ethan and I had agreed that once Ray felt ready to talk about it and seek help that we would support him through it.

We sat in his living room on the sofa as Ethan's mom, Cindy, prepared dinner. She was usually working when we came over, but on her days off, she would always make sure we were well fed. I think she felt bad that she wasn't always around and finding meals was left for us to do. Ethan was used to it, though, so he would typically make us food, which consisted of mac and cheese, sandwiches, and frozen pizza. Ray and I didn't mind; neither of us were too fancy about food. We all just enjoyed each other's company.

"Dinner is ready!" Cindy called out.

We all gathered around the table and thanked her for dinner.

"Ray, I've been meaning to ask you how your mom has been." Cindy asked.

Ray awkwardly shifted in his seat. Ethan mentioned that his Cindy had told him that she and Ray's mom were friends growing up. Ray seemed confused as to how Cindy knew her; I guess his mom never mentioned it.

"You know my mom?" he questioned.

Cindy smiled, "Oh yes! I guess she never mentioned to you, but it was so long ago…she and I, along with Jessica Hale, were all best friends since kindergarten."

Ray stared at her in disbelief, as if the idea that his mom had a life growing up was difficult to believe.

Cindy continued, "We lost track of each other, you know, with your mom getting married right out of high school. I guess she got busy, and then of course she had you and your siblings…"

Ray's mouth dropped open. "My mom got married right after high school to him?"

Cindy looked worried, as if she had been caught saying something she wasn't supposed to. "Uh, yes, I'm sorry I thought you knew. ."

Ray's face turned pale. He looked as if he wasn't sure whether to ask more questions or if he wanted to disappear. Ethan and I exchanged looks. I wondered if his mom had noticed anything about their relationship when they first met...

"H-how's w-work, Mom?" Ethan ejected. His attempt at changing the subject, I guessed.

Cindy rolled her eyes. "It's been okay, except they keep cutting my hours. I only have three shifts this week...oh, I almost forgot!" Cindy jumped up and reached for something on the kitchen counter.

When she sat back down, she held up a brochure in her hand. I read the title on the front page: *Drawing Competition!* With an email listed below for submissions.

"A lady dropped a bunch of these off at the bar, and I knew it was a sign! "Ethan, honey, you have to do this!" Cindy exclaimed.

Ethan's cheeks turned red, and his lips began to quiver, a sign that he was feeling anxious. "I—I don't think I—I'm g-good enough m-mom."

Ray shook his head in protest, "Are you kidding? Your drawings are amazing, man. Why do you think we got an A+ on our English assignment? It wasn't because of the story about a fire-breathing cat that Sam and I came up with." Ray laughed, "It was because of your drawings. I mean, that's why Mrs. Simon suggested you design the yearbook covers for the yearbook this year!"

Oh no. I don't think Cindy knew about that yet. As soon as Ray realized what he said, his eyes widened. Ethan looked like he wanted to crawl into a shell like a turtle. Ray mouthed *"sorry"* to Ethan. It was too late, though; Cindy had already started to cry.

"What? How could you not tell me?" Cindy asked between sniffles. I got up and grabbed a tissue for her; she thanked me and turned her attention back to Ethan. "Honey, I am so proud of you! You must do this; art is your passion!"

Ethan took a deep breath; before he could respond, the house phone began to ring. Cindy stood up to answer it; after a few "okays" and "uh huhs," she hung up.

"I'm sorry, kids, I have to go; I just got called in, and I must take it, especially with the shift cuts lately. Don't worry about cleaning up the kitchen; I'll do it later." She kissed Ethan on the top of his head, waved at us, and headed out the door.

Ethan looked relieved.

"I'm so sorry, Ethan," Ray apologized.

"I-it's okay; I'm sssorry my mom mentioned your momm" Ethan replied.

Ray gritted his teeth. "Yeah, I still can't believe she has been with that monster for so long. How can she stand him? He probably used to hit her back then too—

"Ray froze. In his anger he let it slip; he had never directly stated the abuse before. Ethan and I had just assumed it. I could see his face turn pale and the panic in his eyes. I didn't know what to do. What could we say?

In an attempt to ease his panic, I blurted out, "Don't worry! I have a secret too…I like girls!"

Well, that was smooth.

I held my breath as I waited for a response.

They probably won't ever talk to me again. Just like that I'm going to lose the only friends I have here.

But to my surprise, Ethan said, "I k-know." ."

I turned to him in shock; he continued. "M-Marissa Grace. T-that's the g-girl we pass in the h-hallway bbbetween h-homeroom and sssecond period. I-I nnnotice you looking at her all the t-time. I thinkkk sssshe's your neighbour r-right?"

I nodded, but I was too shocked to speak.

Ray smiled, "Yeah, I've noticed that too. You should talk to her sometime."

This was it; my biggest secret was exposed. And it went so easily?

Suddenly, I could feel my chest begin to open up as if I had been holding my breath this entire time. For once I felt at peace, like I didn't have to hide anymore. My biggest secret was exposed to my two closest friends, and everything is still okay.

"Do your parents know? I guess not based on your face..." Ray noted.

"No, they don't know. "I mean, one day I'll tell them I don't know when," I confirmed.

Then I turned my attention to Ray, "Speaking of my parents, my dad, I could say something. Maybe he could call the police and—"

Ray cut me off, "No! No, please, no. I don't want the police involved. They will split us up. I have a plan, well, kind of. I have an idea for a plan. Once it is ready, we will get out. I just need to be patient."

I didn't like the idea, but he was right about being separated. His siblings were too young to be left under his watch, especially since he isn't an adult. I doubted he would be allowed to live alone with them if his mom refused to leave her husband.

"O-okay, but we can h-help, if you need aaanything" Ethan assured. I nodded in agreement.

"What I need is for you to submit a drawing in that competition," Ray said as he held up the brochure.

"Yes! We can help you pick one if you want." I asked.

Ethan took a second to think about it; he then went into the bedroom and pulled out a stack of about ten sketchbooks.

"F-fine. I guess it's w-wroth a t-try" he said as he put the sketchbooks on the floor.

We spent the rest of the night looking through all of Ethan's drawings.

For the first time in our friendship, we were all authentically ourselves. Leaning on each other for confidence and acceptance. I could tell the boys felt it as well. It was like something clicked in us; we felt brave enough to fully be ourselves, no matter the outcome.

It was the best night of my life.

CHAPTER TEN

ETHAN

Sam invited Ray and me over for dinner; she said her parents had been wanting to have us over to get an opportunity to get to know us and our families better since we usually hung out at my house. My mom had the day off today, so she drove Ray and me over. Ray's mom couldn't come; he told my mom she was busy taking care of Ella and Daniel, though I knew the truth. I don't think his mom is allowed to leave the house often, and when she does, his dad is always close by watching. I don't know how much my mom knew about Ray and his homelife. My mom had mentioned his mom, Lizzy, many times to me growing up; I remember after she and Ray's mom dropped us off on our first day of grade one. They chatted for a few minutes before his dad swiftly interrupted, and then they left in a hurry. At the time I didn't think much of it; I was too young to see the signs. The way my mom looked at Ray made me think that she must have known something; she always had a look of sorrow or regret. As if she could have changed things for him. I never dared to ask her. I didn't want to overstep on Ray's business or my mom's. If she wanted me to know what she had known, she would have said something.

Instead, when Ray made up an excuse that his mom was stuck at home babysitting, my mom commented that she had wished she could have made it as she missed her and was looking forward to reconnecting, but she understood she was busy. She didn't press on the matter any further after that. When we pulled into Sam's house, I noticed a family standing on her front porch. Ray and I exchanged a look. It was Marissa Grace's family.

We got out of the car and waved; Marissa's parents introduced themselves. Marissa smiled at us as she fiddled with her dress, as if she was nervous about something. Then Sam opened the door, and her eyes widened. She immediately brushed her fingers through her curls and let out a nervous "hello! ."

I don't think Sam knew that Marissa and her family were invited over as well.

We walked inside, and Sam's parents came over to greet everyone. I had to admit it was a bit weird being over at the principal's house, but the few times I had visited, he had always been very welcoming. My mom joined Marissa and Sam's mom in the kitchen as they discussed whatever recipe Sam's mom had prepared. Marissa's dad had helped himself to the appetizers on the living room table as Ray and Sam's dad started talking about the latest baseball game. I don't think Ray really watched baseball, but he was good at pretending he did.

Marissa found herself on the couch sipping on a glass of bubbly water. Sam... Well, Sam was nervously checking herself in the dining room mirror. I walked over to her, and as soon as she saw me, she began to panic.

"They invited her over and didn't tell me!" she said as she fixed up her mascara. I couldn't help but smile.

"D-don't worry. Just t-talk to her."

Sam looked at me like what I said was ridiculous. Maybe it was especially coming from me, the guy who only actively talks to three people on a daily basis voluntarily.

Then Marissa made her way into the dining room as well. Sam smiled, looked at me, and blurted out, "Hey Marissa! Thank you for coming tonight. It's really cool to officially meet you. I mean, I have seen you in the hallways at school every day, not in a stalkery way, but like, you know, we always cross paths when I go to my second-period class and you go to your second-period class—"

I think I gave her bad advice.

Marissa giggled, "Yeah, I have seen you around too! I was just wondering where the washroom was," she asked.

Sam gulped and gestured for Marissa to follow her. Hopefully, the longer the night goes on, the more confident Sam will get....

I felt a tap on my shoulder and turned around. Sam's mom smiled and invited me to the kitchen, where my mom and Marissa's mom were all staring at me and smiling. Before I could ask why they were looking at me like that, my mom said, "Ethan! You never told me that Sam was your girlfriend?"

Oh boy.

Where did that come from?

Did Sam tell her parents we were dating? If so, she forgot to tell me about that.

"Hazel told me that she has a theory that you two are secretly dating!" my mom continued as she gestured towards Sam's mom.

The three ladies were looking at me like I was about to announce the final rose on *The Bachelor.* (I watched it with my mom, okay?)

"N-no, Ssam and I are j-just friends." I protested.

Their smiles grew even wider, and Sam's mom patted me on the back. "Oh sure, maybe for now, but I bet you two will be going to the end of the school year dance together!"

It felt like if Sam's mom could hypnotize me into believing that Sam and I were in love, she would.

If only she knew there was someone that Sam had a crush on in this house, but it wasn't me.

Thankfully, dinner was ready, so my interrogation was cut short, and we all sat around the dinner table in the dining room.

As we ate dinner, Sam's dad, who had taken a liking to Ray, asked him about his plans for college. I could tell Ray felt uncomfortable. I don't think he had a plan for college or for anything after school outside of trying to get out of his house. He was a credit behind in

English anyway; he would have to complete that first before he got accepted anywhere.

Ray used that as his excuse: "Um, well, you may know, but I still have to complete grade twelve-level English. So, I don't think I will be applying anywhere yet—"

Sam's dad waved his hand as if it wasn't that big of an issue. "That's okay! You can do summer school, complete the course, apply to places, and enroll in the winter semester. Students do it all the time!" he stated.

Ray nodded as if he was actually considering that option, but I doubted he was. It wasn't a bad idea by any means; it was actually a very good one. I just don't think Ray was ready to think about that yet, which honestly made me sad. He was so worried about his siblings that his own life was on the back burner. I didn't have any siblings or live with a dad like Ray's, so I could never fully understand, but I suppose if I did, I would be doing the same.

Sam and Marissa were constantly looking at each other at opposite times, which I found amusing. As soon as one of the girls would look away, the other would turn their gaze on them. It was like a game of cat and mouse, only I don't think they realized, which made it even more amusing. I'd have to tell Sam later; I think her crush may be crushing on her back. I won't have a date to the dance, but Sam's mom would be ecstatic if she had one. I know Sam was worrying about coming out to her parents, but from what I could tell, her mom was just itching for her to find love, and who knows, maybe she will with Marissa. It sure does look like they both are interested even though they were both too anxious to clue into it.

Ray's cellphone ringing snapped me out of my thoughts. He apologized and quickly walked into the living room to answer it. A knot grew in my stomach. Ray had told us that the only person who calls him on his cellphone is Daniel to report an emergency. Sam and I locked eyes, clearly thinking the same thing.

Judging by Ray's face, something was certainly wrong.

Ray hung up the phone and stumbled over in a panic, as if he had just awoken from a nightmare.

"I—I need to go right now," his voice sounded hoarse, like he was holding in a scream.

"Ella is in the hospital."

CHAPTER ELEVEN

RAY

The ride to the hospital was the longest fifteen minutes of my life. Daniel's voice rang repeatedly through my head: "Ella is bleeding; we're taking her to the hospital." Come quick!

I was so angry I could kill that monster.

Cindy was driving as fast as she could. Ethan sat in the backseat. Nobody had said a word the entire drive. I didn't mind. I was too busy worrying to think about talking to anyone. I just wanted to get there and make sure she was okay. The amount of anxiety bubbling in my stomach made me nauseous.

When we arrived at the hospital, I quickly thanked Cindy and flung the car door open. I almost forgot to close it as I was preoccupied with the need to run inside the hospital doors. As I entered the emergency room, I quickly scanned around, looking for Ella or Daniel. That's when I noticed the police officers talking to Daniel in an office room at the back of the emergency floor.

Why were they talking to Daniel? Did he expose what was going on at home?

For a second, I felt free; if he had, maybe something could be done, and we could finally escape him. But then I remembered that Mom would never leave him and would probably try her best to defend him. It wouldn't be that easy.

I noticed the monster sitting in the waiting area on his phone; his knees were shaking, but not from worry. He wouldn't care. He was probably just itching for a beer. I was surprised he was here; I expected him to be at the bar, hiding out until we got back. I was about to walk over to him and punch him in the face, but the sound of Ella calling my name snapped me out of my rage.

I turned and saw her and Mom in one of the small rooms where they put you as you wait for the doctor. She had a big gash along her forehead underneath a pack of ice. I ran to her and gave her a hug.

"What happened?!" I demanded, "What did he do to her?"

That's when Mom said the unthinkable, "Daniel threw a glass dinner plate at her; they were fighting over who got to watch TV, and..."

I couldn't believe it. Daniel, who never got involved in any conflict and doesn't even know how to form a fist, would never hurt anyone. Especially not Ella. She was lying. Covering for that monster. It made sense now why Daniel was talking to the police and why that monster was in the waiting room. They lied. Blamed it on Daniel so he took the heat. Meanwhile, the monster was just around to make sure everybody got their scripts right. I looked at Ella, who avoided my gaze. She was young, but she understood that whatever the monster says goes; she knew that going against his rules meant bad things would happen at home.

Daniel. They couldn't arrest him, could they? He wasn't even a teenager yet. He was just a kid. I hoped the police officers wouldn't buy the fake story; maybe they would notice the signs and investigate the monster instead. I couldn't believe my mom would do this. I knew she was blindly in love with that monster, but after this? Blaming everything on one of her children...it wasn't fair. She was just as bad as he was. Maybe even worse.

Before I could yell at my mom out of frustration, a blonde woman entered the room. I read her nametag: *Jessica Hale, Social Worker.* I remembered Ethan's mom, Cindy, mentioning that name a while ago; she mentioned that Jessica Hale, my mom, and she were friends growing up. Judging by the look on my mom's face, she was definitely the same Jessica that I heard of.

I couldn't tell if my mom was happy or worried to see Jessica. Jessica quickly scanned whatever was on her clipboard before she looked up and smiled at us.

"Hello, Lizzy, it's nice to see you again, but I'm very sorry it's under these circumstances," Jessica noted.

All my mom managed to do was nod. Jessica then turned her attention to Ella.

"You are so pretty!" Ella said as she smiled up at Jessica.

Jessica chuckled, "Thank you so much, sweetie. So are you! Wow, you look so much like your mommy did when she was your age." Jessica examined the wound on her forehead. "I heard you and your brother Daniel got into a little argument at home, huh?" she asked.

Ella looked at me carefully, then at my mom. I noticed my mom holding Ella's leg tightly, as if she was holding onto her lifeline. It was a signal; stick to the script.

Ella nodded, and before she began to speak, I heard whispering in the waiting room. When I looked, I saw Daniel being escorted back to the monster with a police officer by his side. He didn't have any handcuffs on, so that was a good sign. I left the room and walked towards them, eager to hear what was going on.

"We had a good talk with Daniel here." The police officer stated as he patted him on the back, "We have agreed to not charge him with anything due to him being a minor, but we have suggested anger management classes. Daniel has taken some informative brochures about different options you can decide on as a family," the police officer smiled.

I was happy that Daniel wasn't getting in any real trouble, but I still felt sick to my stomach over the situation.

The monster cleared his throat and shook the police officer's hand. "Thank you, boys. I promise we will talk about this at home. He definitely needs to work on his anger management skills. Thank you for talking some sense into him; hopefully, he takes this lesson into consideration in the future. "

Are you kidding me? Daniel is the one who needs to work on his anger.

If we weren't in a hospital surrounded by police officers, I would've thrown him into a wall by now.

Maybe I needed to look at those brochures.

The police officers left the building; the monster then returned to his seat without a word.

I looked at Daniel; he was visibly shaking, gripping those stupid brochures so hard it looked like they were stuck to his hands with glue. I wanted to ask him if he was okay, but it was clear he wasn't ready to talk yet, so I let him sit down in peace. When I looked towards Ella's room, I noticed Jessica Hale leaving as a doctor walked in. When Jessica saw me, she walked over to us.

"Hello, I just wanted to inform you that Dr. James will be stitching up Ella's wound, and then you will be on your way. There have been no signs of concussion." She informed us.

The monster didn't even look up from his phone, no surprise there.

'Thank you very much for updating us," I said.

Jessica nodded; when we locked eyes, it felt like she could look into my soul. Like she knew all my secrets. Cindy looked at me the same way. Almost like we were in a secret club, knowing something so dark, but there was nothing we could do about it. They must know. I wonder if there were times when they begged my mom to leave that monster as well. I had so many things I wanted to ask the two of them, but I didn't dare to.

Deep down I was terrified of the answers.

****

The monster spent the car ride home complaining about how he was late to beer night with his buddies. As if every night wasn't beer night for him. He had no regard for the pain he had caused Ella or Daniel. Mom was quietly apologizing to him, as if she overreacted for bringing Ella to the hospital.

I wanted to kill him.

I searched for something in the car to use as a weapon. There were lots of empty beer bottles and fast food wrappers, and then I noticed it.

A baseball bat tucked underneath the driver's seat in front of me. I stared at it as I came up with a plan. Daniel, who was sitting in the middle seat, lightly tapped his leg against mine. I looked at him, and he followed my gaze to the baseball bat. He could tell what I was planning. He shook his head at me, warning me to leave it alone. But I couldn't. How could I?

As soon as we pulled into the driveway, I was ready for my plan to unfold.

The monster grumbled for us to get out of his truck so he could drive to the bar. My mom got out, unbuckled Ella from her car seat, and walked towards the front door with Daniel trailing behind her. He glared at me from the rearview mirror.

"Can't you hear, idiot?" I said, "Get out!" he demanded.

So, I did. He didn't notice me taking the baseball bat with me.

At Sam's parents' house, Principal Meyers was talking to me about baseball.

I never thought I was a fan of baseball…until now.

Mom's screams travelled from the front door as I slammed the baseball bat into his driver's side window.

The rage was so strong inside of me it was almost as if I blacked out. I just kept smashing everything I could reach—the windows, the doors, and the tires.

Then he managed to get out of the truck.

So, I began to smash the baseball bat into him.

Mom was still screaming, but I was so tuned into my rage that I tuned her out completely. It wasn't until he got ahold of my arm, and I dropped the baseball bat, that I could hear her clearly again.

He threw me into his truck, hard. I looked up and saw Ella and Daniel watching from the living room window. Mom was running up to us, flailing her arms in protest.

"Stop! Please! He is just a boy," she begged.

The monster punched me in the stomach again and again before tossing me to the ground.

He spat at me before mumbling, "I'm going to walk to the bar; when I come back, all this damn mess better be cleaned up!" Then he began to walk away.

Mom helped me up and brought me inside the kitchen. She searched in the fridge for an ice pack for my stomach. Even though she tried to help me, I was still in rage mode. I couldn't forgive her that easily. So, I started to yell at her.

"This is your fault! How many times have I begged you to leave him? How many times has he hit you, hit us! This isn't fair! We shouldn't have to live like this. I should be worrying about college or girls or homework! Instead, I'm constantly worrying about how to keep us safe. That's not my job! That's your job!" I couldn't stop; I kept going. Letting out everything I had been holding onto for as long as I could remember. "Ethan's mom, Cindy, told me that you married that monster when you were practically my age. You had years and years to see the signs and leave. But you didn't! And if you were okay with this life, fine, good for you! But your kids shouldn't have to suffer with you. You should have given us away or something. We didn't deserve to suffer just because you fell in love with the Devil!"

Tears were streaming down her face. I was feeling a mixture of guilt and freedom. Part of me knew that she was a victim like the rest of us. She cared enough to protect us as best as she could if he ever targeted one of us. I could see the panic in her eyes whenever the monster would turn to me, Daniel, or Ella. But I was still angry at her. I was angry at her choice to stay with him despite all of the pain that he had caused. I couldn't understand how she hadn't tried to escape by now, how she never tried to tell anyone. I knew why I couldn't; I didn't want us to get split up. It would've been easier for her, though; all she had to do was take us and run. Run somewhere he could never find us. I doubt he would even try to find us if we ever did escape; he would probably just look for another poor woman to prey on. We weren't people to him, just punching bags to let out all of his ugly demons on. I felt lighter after I began to calm down. I noticed that it felt easier to breathe; my mind didn't feel as clouded with anxiety. Being able to fully let my feelings out felt therapeutic; finally, my pain wasn't isolated in my heart anymore. The pain was let out of the cage in my mind, where it had been locked up for my entire life.

My mom handed me an ice pack with shaking hands. I noticed her eyes looked around for Daniel and Ella. They weren't anywhere to be found; Daniel probably took her to her room once I started to yell so she could be sheltered from it. He was good at his role of keeping her away from the violence, even when I got involved.

I noticed my mom begin to dig into her sweater pocket and pull something out of it. She opened up the palm of her hand and moved it closer to me. I looked at what she was holding and noticed a small plastic bag with pills inside it.

She looked up at me, her eyes full of determination and anger that I had never seen in her before.

"I'm sorry, Raymond. You are right. It is my job to protect you all. You have done a great job all of these years..." She put her hand on my face, "but it's my turn to step up now."

I looked down at the bag of pills in her other hand, and a wave of questions ran through my mind. Where did she get them from? Did Jessica give them to her? What was she planning? It was clear that she was ready to seek revenge. I just hoped that her plan was solid; she couldn't afford to make any mistakes. Mistakes in this situation would mean death, not just for her, but for us all.

CHAPTER TWELVE

ETHAN

I hadn't stopped staring at the envelope since I returned home from the mailbox. There were two options for what was inside of it: option one, they had received my submission for the art competition, and I did not win. Maybe they would send along a ribbon that says, "Good Job!" or some other lame way of telling you that your submission sucked. Option two: the judges somehow actually liked my submission, and I had won the competition. which was the less likely option of the two. There was no way that the piece that I had submitted could have beaten everyone else that applied. There were probably hundreds of artists with more experience than me, better quality supplies, and maybe even a personal mentor that they could afford to teach them the newest and greatest trends in the art world.

The piece that I had selected with the help of Ray, Sam, and my mom was one that I wouldn't have picked without their encouragement. Honestly, it was so personal to me that I had almost backed out of submitting it, but my mom was able to convince me to send it in and take the risk. The painting was of me as a young boy, on my first day of kindergarten. A memory burnt in my brain so strongly that I did not even need to reference a photo of my old school or what I was wearing in order to duplicate it perfectly. I remember my mom had given me the typical bowl-cut haircut because it was cheaper than paying the back-to-school prices that the salons would have charged us. I wore jean overalls with a red and white striped t-shirt underneath. I was playing on the playground by the sandbox when I attempted to ask another kid in my class for the bucket. I had a stutter then, and until that day I had only really been around my mom. She never judged me; of course, she would try to work with me on how to pronounce things the 'right' way, but she never made me feel like my voice was something to be ashamed of. This was the first time where I was left to speak without her around; I didn't know it, but it was about to be something that I would never forget. I remember the look the little girl gave me after I had asked her to borrow the bucket; she immediately pointed at me and asked, "Why is your voice like that?" I was confused; I knew my words came out differently than hers did, but I never compared myself to the other kids until that moment. The girl then made matters more humiliating by calling over some of the kids who were playing in the yard with us. "Come here! You need to listen to Ethan talk; he sounds so funny!" By this time we had about five other little kindergarteners surrounding us. I could feel the embarrassment making my cheeks flush; the anxiety pumped through my chest. Whenever I felt nervous, which was often, especially when I had to speak in front of anyone new, my stuttering would increase, and I could feel the words struggle to come out of my mouth even more. The little kids stared at me, waiting for me to do something 'funny' like how people surround animals while they're standing on the other side of the glass in a zoo. I was too nervous to speak, and before I could even try, I had peed my pants.

The kids all began to laugh; the teacher came over and helped guide me to the washroom with the change of clothing my mom had packed in my backpack. It was the first time I had ever been told that my voice was different, or funny, as the girl had stated. It was the first time that I had ever felt different from everyone else in the world, and it was a lesson that I would never forget. The painting was of that moment, me playing in the sandbox as the little girl pointed at me and the other kids surrounded me in curiosity. The painting of my face included a white cloth covering my mouth, with red lettering on it that read "different."

I had kept that painting in a closet in the laundry room with some of my other artwork. I had never shown anyone the painting before, not even my mom. It felt like being naked. It was too personal and too emotional to share with my mom; I didn't want to see her happy memory of my first day of school get transformed into a memory so painful. So, when Sam had started to dig through the closet to look at the artwork I had stored there, I immediately panicked. She and Ray admired what was in the box and would give me compliments on each piece that they discovered, but then they pulled out that one. We sat in silence for a few minutes; I noticed Sam wipe a tear away from her eye when she thought I wasn't looking. Ray was the first to speak, calling it heartbreakingly beautiful. He said if I was comfortable enough with it, that this would be the painting he would choose for me to send out. I couldn't believe it at first; who would even care about it? It wasn't a universal piece of art that many people could relate to or admire, like an animal or a flower. Sam agreed with him; I told them I needed to think about it.

When my mom got home that night, she had noticed it sitting on the living room table. I heard her sobs from the bedroom; they were so heavy that they woke me up from my sleep. I went to the living room and saw her holding the painting with one hand and wiping her eyes with a tissue in the other.

"This... this was your first day of kindergarten," she stated. "I remember your outfit; it was my favourite on you. You looked so handsome and adorable. I remember your teacher told me you had an accident while playing outside, so she had to send you to change your clothes... I just assumed you weren't used to being away from me and your nerves caused you to soil yourself. I didn't...didn't think that it could've been because you were being bullied? Oh, my goodness, honey, you were so young I didn't think kids would notice anything at that age."

I didn't want her to feel guilty; I knew this would happen if she had ever seen the painting. Without thinking I took it out of her hands and headed for the kitchen garbage.

"Wait, Ethan, what are you doing?" she asked.

"I'm sssorry m-mom, you weren't sssupposed to ever see t-this. I shouldn't hhhave even made it in the ffirst place. Sssam and Ray wwwanted me to sssubmit it in that c-contest but it's just ssstupid." I told her as I got closer to the garbage can.

My mom surprised me by running towards me and reaching for the painting before I could throw it out. "Don't you dare throw this out! It is beautiful. It is honest and it is your reality. While it may not have been the picture-perfect moment, it was the truth, your truth. And you should never hide yourself from anyone. You have nothing to be ashamed of; yes, you are different. But so is everybody! Some people have long hair, some have no hair, some are tall, some are short, some have accents, and some stutter." She touched my hair lovingly. "We are all different, and that's what makes us special. Don't hide your light from the world, honey; you are beautiful, and the world deserves to see you embrace your shine!"

Something hit me in that moment; I decided to listen to my mom's advice. No more hiding my artwork in closets; I was willing to take a risk and put myself and my art into the world. If I didn't win the contest, then that would be okay with me, but maybe it would give me the confidence to someday become the artist that I had always dreamed of being.

I slowly opened up the envelope and slid open the folded paper inside of it. I held my breath as I read the message:

Congratulations! Ethan Suzuki, you have been selected as the contest winner! Please attend the art gallery on July 11, 2026. Bring your original piece with you to have it displayed in the art gallery amongst the past contest winners throughout the years. We are looking forward to seeing you at the art gallery. If you have any questions, please contact us directly.

I actually did it. I won!

CHAPTER THIRTEEN

SAM

The last day of school dance theme was Under the Sea. My dad chose it for me, knowing my love for everything underwater related. It was a sweet gesture, but I didn't want him announcing that to the school; that would have been embarrassing. The social committee members decorated the gym with blue wallpaper and clear balloons to pose as bubbles, and Ethan was elected to design all of the underwater animal drawings along the walls and the stage. When my dad had heard that Ethan had won the art contest, he immediately elected him to design the art for all future school events; I don't think Ethan minded though. Since the day he got the news, he had a new wave of confidence about him when it came to his art; he even felt comfortable enough to hang up some of his artwork around his house, including the piece that he had won the competition with. He was walking along the perimeter of the gym with my dad as he showcased all his work; my dad looked increasingly amazed with each design. Personally, the life-sized shark on the back wall was my favourite. I noticed Ray by the snack and punch table, so I walked over to greet him. He was wearing an oversized white dress shirt that my dad had given him to wear and a pair of blue jeans. He seemed distracted ever since the incident happened with Ella. He never fully explained what had happened that night, just that Ella got hurt and was feeling better. I couldn't help but think there was more going on, but Ethan and I didn't want to push him; we knew that talking about his home life was a difficult subject for Ray.

Ray gave me a head nod and gestured towards the art that Ethan had made. "Look at our boy go, huh? He did amazing!"

I smiled, "I know. I was expecting him to decline when my dad asked him to design the dance art, but he actually seemed super excited about it. Hopefully he keeps making stuff during the summer; maybe he could even sell some of his stuff too?"

"Yeah, we could totally set up a garage sale or something like that for him to display his stuff at," Ray added. "He is super talented; maybe even some art person could sign him at the art gallery next week, or however that works."

He kept saying stuff, but I wasn't listening; I was distracted by Marissa walking in. She looked so beautiful. Her red hair was in waves, and her bangs were clipped up with blue seashell clips; she had a matching blue mermaid-style dress on. She was like a real-life Ariel from *Little Mermaid.* I guess I must have been staring at Marissa for so long that even Ray noticed and nudged me.

"You should go ask her to dance; I think she likes you," Ray noted.

I rolled my eyes. "No way!" I could feel my cheeks burning just by the thought of dancing with her.

Ethan and Ray had this theory that Marissa liked me; apparently at my parents' dinner party we both kept looking at each other without the other noticing. I didn't trust them completely; I mean, it's a known fact that boys are clueless. How could they notice something like that and I didn't? My theory was that the boys just wanted me to embarrass myself because they were too involved in me finding love, much like my mom.

Ray winked at me and then walked away. Before I could ask him where he was going, I noticed Marissa walking up to me. *She was probably just heading for the food or the punch*, I thought. There was no way she was actually coming over just to talk to me...

Hey Sam! "I really love your mermaid dress; it looks stunning on you," Marissa said as she touched one of the shiny sequins on my hip. I felt so warm that I was worried I was about to burst into flames right then and there.

"T-thank you. I really love the blue seashells in your hair, very creative! I love everything underwater; it is so fascinating—" I managed to stop myself before I continued blubbering away. What was it about this girl that turned me into an oversharing puddle of anxiety?

Marissa laughed, "That's pretty cool; I loved watching *Finding Nemo* growing up. my favourite were the turtles."

Then I blurted out, "I have a turtle named Gary! He is in my room; you should come see him sometime!" Oh my goodness, I was blowing it.

Marissa smiled ecstatically. "Really! I would love that. Are you free tomorrow?"

Was this really happening, was Marissa Grace asking to come to my house, to my room, to meet my turtle...?

I cleared my throat before responding, "Totally, I'm free; come whenever you want!" Okay, that didn't sound that bad.

Before I could think of something else to add, Marissa grabbed my hand. "Do you want to go dance?"

Marissa Grace was asking me to dance with her.

I must be dreaming.

I looked around the gym and noticed Ethan and Ray smiling at me from the sidelines of the dance floor. Ethan gave me a thumbs up, and Ray made kissing faces at me. I didn't have brothers, but with them I now have a good idea of what they would be like. I ignored them and followed Marissa to the dance floor.

The night went by in a flash; Marissa and I spent the entire time dancing together and laughing and talking. I found out that she loves to knit, and she even created her own blog about it. How cute! She also moved to town a couple years ago, so she was relatively new as well. The biggest thing that she revealed to me was that she had broken up with her girlfriend a year ago due to long distance not working out between them.

Marissa Grace had a girlfriend. Marissa Grace likes girls.

And when she kissed me, I realized the best fact of all.

Marissa Grace liked me.

I was so lost in shock and happiness that I had almost forgotten where we were. That we were at a school dance in the school gym where my dad worked. When I suddenly remembered, I pulled away, and my eyes darted around looking for my dad. Dread crept up inside my stomach; I prayed that he had returned to his office and had gotten bored of watching the students dance and drink fruit punch.

But then I saw him, on the stage beside another teacher who was supervising the dance. Maybe he didn't, see? I thought, but the look in his eyes as he stared back at me said otherwise.

Marissa Grace and I just kissed, and my dad saw.

CHAPTER FOURTEEN

RAY

I was so proud of Sam for actually getting the confidence to talk to Marissa, and then she even danced with her all night long, but the best part was the kiss. Ethan was finally embracing his inner artist; Sam was finally finding love. As my best friends were growing up, I felt like a proud parent in a TV show.

It's been a week since Ella's hospital visit. The monster had bought a brand-new truck after he sold the old one for parts. I guess I did too much damage for him to bother fixing; oops. I wasn't sure what Mom was waiting for; she had the extra pills. All she needed to do was mix them in his beer or his food, and surely something bad would happen. Jessica had told her that overdosing on that medication was known to cause severe complications, including heart failure. I was surprised to learn that Jessica even stole pills from the hospital for my mom; that was risky for someone to do. My mom had told me that she finally got the courage to ask for help, but she was too afraid for it to go wrong; apparently, she had tried before, and the police officers didn't believe her. She was sent back to him as if she was a delusional housewife; my dad blamed it on her pregnancy hormones. So, Jessica did what any childhood best friend would do; she stole pills from her work in hopes that my mom was finally ready to leave that monster for good.

In the back of my head, I was worried, worried that she would change her mind, and we would never be free from the cycle of his wrath. But I tried my best to have faith that my mom really meant what she had said to me that night. Each time I had come home, I half expected police cars and ambulances to be carrying the monster away in a body bag. It hasn't happened yet, but I was hopeful that someday soon it would.

After the dance had ended, Sam quickly ran up to Ethan and me and demanded that we had to leave in a hurry. I wasn't sure what she was worried about, and then I remembered that her dad was a chaperone tonight. Did he see them kiss? I hoped not. Mr. Meyers was a kind man, and I didn't think he would ever not accept Sam, but Sam hadn't come out to her parents yet, and I didn't think that a situation like that would be how she imagined that moment to be. Sam led us into the hallway and outside the exit door, where we were greeted by two police officers that were making their way up the steps towards us.

One of the police officers put his hand out to stop us. "Sorry, kids, we are looking for someone. Do you know Raymond Martinez?"

I could feel Sam's and Ethan's eyes on me.

"Yes, that's me. Why?" I asked.

The police officers looked at each other, and the one who had stopped us spoke up, "We need you to come

with us, please; there has been an incident in your home.
".

"What happened? Are my siblings okay?" I asked.

Then the officer said something that I hadn't expected, "Your mother has been shot; she is in the hospital. We have come to pick you up and ask you some questions regarding your father. ".

That's when I blacked out.

The next thing that I had remembered was arriving at the hospital. The police officers led me to the same room that Daniel was questioned in the week before. I looked around for Daniel and Ella when I walked in, but I didn't see them. I didn't see the monster either. Maybe they had arrested him, or maybe he fled and got away. A tall doctor walked in and whispered something to the police officers that I couldn't hear and then walked back out. I couldn't help but wonder if he had just told them that my mom had died. One of the police officers left the room, so it was just me and the one who did all of the talking back at school. I wondered what Sam and Ethan were thinking right now.

The police officer offered me a glass of water, but I was too anxious to accept it. Then, he began to explain the situation to me. I didn't realize it, but I had held my breath the entire time he was speaking to me.

"Raymond, my name is Officer Torres, as I mentioned earlier." I didn't even remember him introducing himself to me, so it must have been after my brain had frozen. "My partner and I got a call that your brother Daniel had called 9-1-1 to report a shooting in your home. He stated that your father Paul Martinez had gotten upset during dinner and shot your mother Elizabeth Martinez. When the paramedics arrived on scene, they saw your mother on the ground in your kitchen, and your father was lying on the floor unresponsive. It appears that he had suffered an overdose. It looks like he had some panic or confusion while he was overdosing and may have shot her by accident. Is he a heavy drug user?"

So, she did drug him, but he noticed. I didn't even know he had a gun anywhere; he had never mentioned it. I guess he kept it hidden and didn't want to give me any ideas. Did my mom know about it? Maybe if she had, she wouldn't have attempted to do this if she had known.

I nodded to the officer to confirm. "Yes, my dad did drink a lot; he did drugs often too. I guess he overestimated his limit this time..."

The officer offered me the glass of water again before he continued, "Your mom is being looked at by the doctors now; the bullet hit her in the right shoulder, but she is stable and looks like she will make it just fine," he assured me, "but your father, he didn't make it to the hospital. He passed away in the ambulance while en route here."

He was dead. The monster was dead. I tried my best to contain a smile. I was so happy I had to fight the urge to get up from the chair and start dancing or singing or praying, maybe all three.

The officer continued, "When we had searched your home, we noticed a pretty decent-sized duffle bag in what we were told was your closet. I opened it and saw some food, clothing, and passports for you and your siblings. Were you planning a trip?"

Was I now a suspect?

I decided to tell the truth; he was dead now, so what did it matter? "I kept that stuff in case we needed to run away. Home wasn't the best environment, as you can gather," I replied.

The officer nodded and then reached for something in his brief case on the floor. When he placed it on the table, I saw three large plastic bags with *"Evidence"* written over them. Inside held one book that looked like a journal in each bag. He took one of them out of the plastic bag and opened it. At first, I wasn't sure what I was looking at; it was journal entries with Polaroid photos of a woman's body covered in bruises or cuts. Each photo had its own entry with the date, time, and a description of what had happened. It wasn't until I looked at the top corner of each page when I noticed a name, Elizabeth Martinez. This was my mom's journal. I was in shock. I had never seen my mom have any journals around before or even a camera. She must have had a hiding spot that she kept secret from me and from him too.

The officer began to explain what I had pieced together: "My partner found these in a compartment above the light fixture in your parents' bedroom ceiling.

It looks like your mother has been collecting evidence on your father's abuse for the last seventeen years. Judging by your age since the time you were born. There were many more journals like these three hidden as well. It was too bad that she didn't bring these forward earlier; we could have arrested that sick prick and saved you kids and your mom a whole lot of trouble. If your dad wasn't in a body bag right now, we would have been taking him away in handcuffs instead. Talk about divine intervention, huh?" he said, and then he winked at me.

He packed up the plastic bags and told me to take all the time I needed to process everything before visiting my mother and my siblings in her hospital room. I thought about those journals, about how many years my mom had been secretly documenting everything. I wondered why she didn't turn them in any sooner, but maybe after the first time she tried to turn him in went south, she was too afraid of the consequences if that had happened again. I was wrong about my mom; she wasn't as devoted to him as she seemed to be. She was just as trapped as we all were by him, until now.

When I arrived at my mom's hospital room, Daniel and Ella greeted me with a hug so tight I thought I was going to vomit up all of the chips and fruit punch that I had consumed at the dance, but I didn't mind. I was just happy to see them safe for once in their lives. My mom was lying in her hospital bed; despite the tubes in her arms, she looked okay. I was expecting worse considering the horror she had just been through.

"How was the dance?" she asked.

I couldn't help but chuckle, "It was cool, but certainly not as exciting as your night was."

She laughed. It was the most beautiful sound that I had ever heard. In my entire life I could never remember a time where she had laughed like that, so free and so content.

Someone knocked on the door; it was Jessica.

She smiled at us as she walked to my mom's bedside. "Hey everyone, I know you all have had a long night, but we have some extra rooms for you three kids to stay in tonight, and it is looking like your mom will be released at the end of the week, so very good news. ".

My mom grabbed Jessica's hands and thanked her for her help. Jessica smiled at her and looked back at my siblings and me. "I'm glad you three are okay. You have a very strong mom; trust me, everything will be okay. You are safe now. ".

It all felt too good to be true. Part of me was waiting for the monster to barge in like in a creepy thriller movie where the bad guy fakes his death and gets away with it in the end. But this wasn't a movie, and he was dead.

We were finally safe.

CHAPTER FIFTEEN

ETHAN

I didn't expect the art gallery to be so busy, but it was full less than thirty minutes after it opened with a large lineup that backed up all the way into the parking lot. My mom, Sam, and Ray had helped me set up my booth. At first it was intimidating, but the more people came by my booth, the easier it felt. I couldn't believe the amount of praise all of these strangers had for me; people I would have never thought to talk to would ask me questions about the painting or about my process. Somehow, even though they were strangers, I didn't feel embarrassed to speak to them, stutter and all. This was me; stuttering was part of my world and part of what made my art special, making me special as well.

Ray and my mom walked side by side, admiring the other booths, occasionally looking back at me and giving me thumbs-up of encouragement. Luckily Ray's mom was getting out of the hospital tomorrow, so he was very happy about that. Now that his dad was gone, Ray was finally able to think about himself and what he wanted out of his own life. He ended up taking Mr. Meyers' advice and signed up for grade twelve English in summer school. He was thinking about applying for the social work program in the winter. I was happy for him; he was finally taking control of his own life.

My mom had been visiting his mom, Lizzy, at the hospital each day and bringing her food and clothes to wear. I was glad she finally had her friend back; I knew she and Jessica had missed her dearly all of these years. Sam and Marissa were walking around the gallery hand in hand with their parents trailing behind them. Sam talked to her parents the night of the dance; she was finally confident enough to come out to them, especially since her dad had already found out her secret. She figured she had nothing to lose. Her mom was ecstatic! She was just happy that Sam had found love; she didn't care about the gender of her soulmate. Her dad seemed happy about it too, though I think he was slightly confused as he thought the two of us were dating. I guess her mom told him that theory of hers too.

For the first time since the three of us had become friends, we were all living lives authentically as ourselves, not held back by the fears and anxieties of our pasts. We weren't outcasts anymore who were isolated by our fears; we were a strong united group of friends who encouraged each other to be ourselves and follow our dreams. I looked forward to our futures; maybe Sam and Marissa would get married, maybe Ray would end up working at the hospital like Jessica, and maybe I would become a famous artist.

Who knows? But what I do know is that whatever happens we will have each other to lean on forever.

Sincerely.

Ethan, Sam, and Ray

P.S. Always embrace your shine. The world is better when you do.